A GLUTEN-FREE BIRTHDAY FOR ME!

By Sue Fliess

Illustrated by Jennifer E. Morris

ALBERT WHITMAN & COMPANY
Chicago, Illinois

To my amazing writing group,
for helping me bake this delicious book
—S.F.

To Mom, and to everyone who has to make sure
they read the ingredients list
—J.E.M.

A note about gluten allergies

Having a food allergy is very common nowadays, but that doesn't mean it's any easier for kids to handle. A food allergy can make a child feel left out of day-to-day activities but especially so at parties. Thankfully, with so many ways to make delicious, gluten-free food today, everyone can enjoy these treats without having to be defined by their allergies or feeling different from their friends.

For more information about gluten allergies, including tips and resources, please see the pages at the end of this book.

It's my birthday...

I can't wait!
Time for us to celebrate!

House is ready,
set for fun.
Cake's the last thing, then we're done.

Can't use flour,
can't eat wheat...
That's got gluten! What's to eat?

Search the cookbooks...
time to bake—
chocolate-cookie-crumble cake!

Guests arriving,
games begin.
Relay races, who will win?

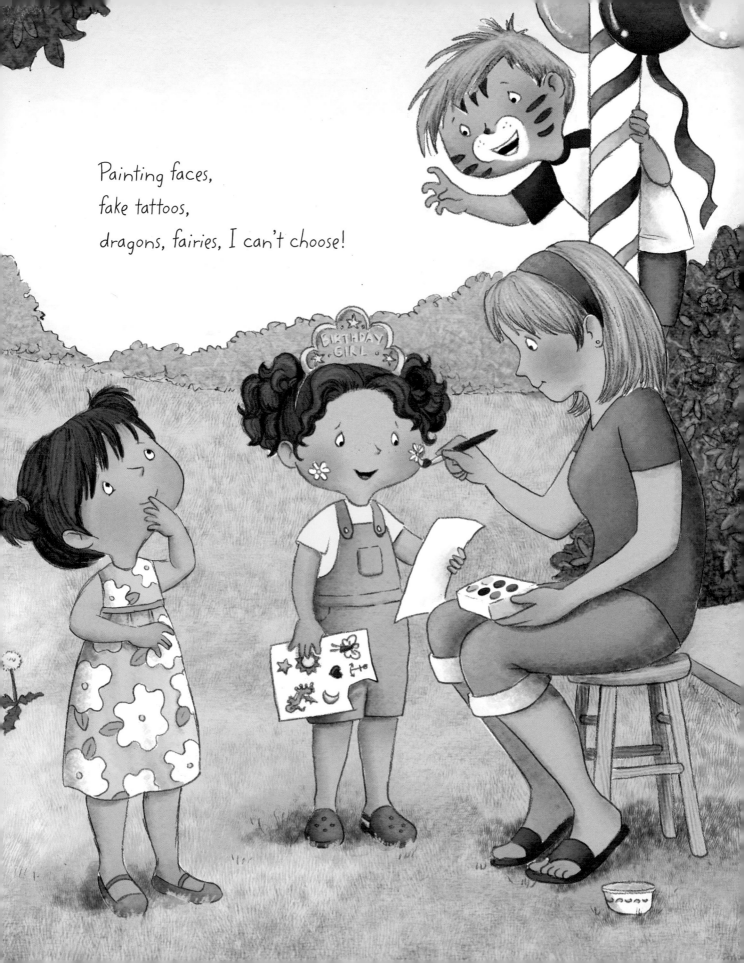

Painting faces,
fake tattoos,
dragons, fairies, I can't choose!

Mom yells, "Cake time!"
We all dash.
Candles flicker, cameras flash.

Wait a minute...
Someone's gone...
Sitting sadly on the lawn.

"Don't you want some?
It tastes good."
He says, "I sure wish I could.

Can't have gluten.
Can't eat cake,
gives me such a tummy ache."

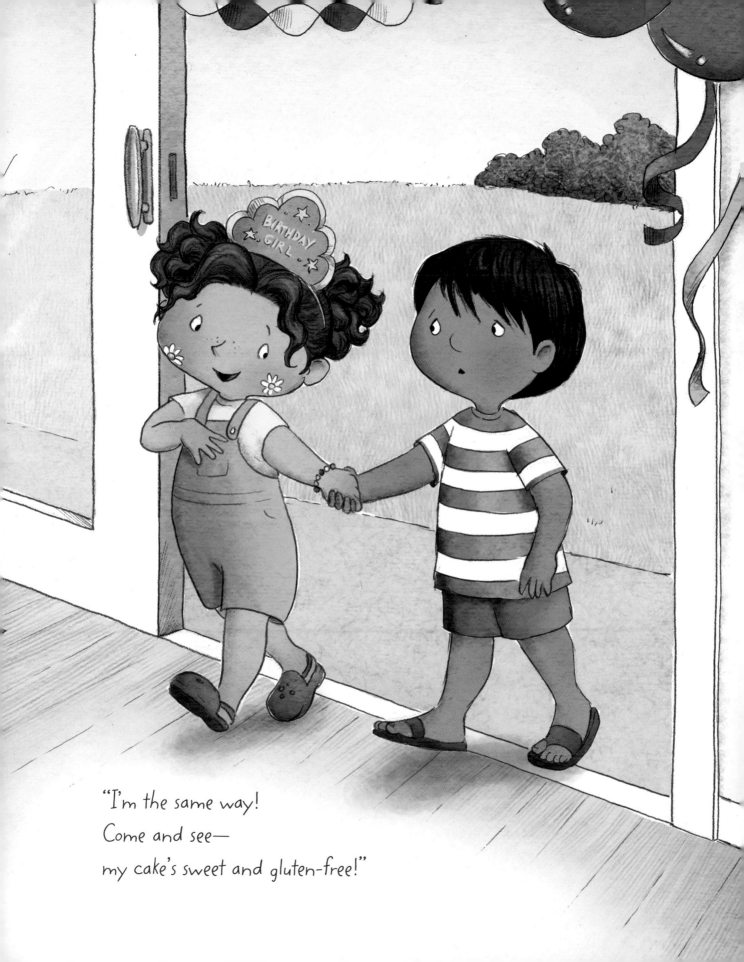

"I'm the same way!
Come and see—
my cake's sweet and gluten-free!"

Friends are singing,
what's my wish?
Hope the crumble cake's delish!

"Cake is yummy!"
"We want more!"
"Did they bake it at the store?"

"Nope, we made it.
Icing too.
Wasn't all that hard to do."

Open presents,
thank my friends.
Party favors...party ends.

Guests are leaving.
Wave good-bye...

Next year we'll make ice-cream pie!

Chocolate-Cookie-Crumble Cake

16 Servings

INGREDIENTS:

2 cups gluten-free all-purpose
flour (Maninis)

1 cup white sugar

1 cup dark brown sugar

3/4 cup unsweetened cocoa
powder

1 teaspoon baking powder

1 teaspoon salt

1 teaspoon ground cinnamon

1/2 cup water

1/2 cup brewed decaf coffee
(don't worry, it doesn't give a
coffee taste!)

1 cup coconut oil

2 teaspoons vanilla extract

a few of your favorite gluten-free
cookies (optional)

DIRECTIONS:

Preheat oven to 350 °F.

In a large bowl, stir together the flour, sugars, cocoa powder, baking powder, salt, and cinnamon. Pour in water, coffee, coconut oil, and vanilla; mix until blended well.

Spread evenly in a 9 x 13 inch baking pan or spoon into mini-muffin pans filling each cup three quarters of the way.

Bake for 20–25 minutes in the baking pan or 12–15 minutes in the mini-muffin pans. If desired, crumble your favorite gluten-free cookies on top while cake is still warm. Let cool on wire rack in pans for at least 10 minutes before cutting into squares (if using the baking pan) or removing from the mini-muffin pans.

Very Berry Pie with Ice Cream
8 Servings

INGREDIENTS:

Filling:

4 cups fresh or frozen mixed
  berries (blueberries,
  raspberries, black-
  berries, strawberries)

1/2 cup sugar

2 tablespoons lemon juice

2 tablespoons tapioca starch

1 teaspoon vanilla extract

1 teaspoon ground cinnamon

Topping:

1/4 cup unsalted butter _or_ coconut
  oil melted

1 cup gluten-free rolled oats
  (Bob's Red Mill)

1/2 cup gluten-free all-purpose flour
  (Maninis)

1/2 cup dark brown sugar

1 teaspoon salt

1/2 teaspoon ground cinnamon

gluten-free ice cream to serve

DIRECTIONS:

Preheat oven to 375 °F.

In a large bowl, stir together the berries, sugar, lemon juice, tapioca starch, vanilla, and cinnamon. Spread evenly in a 9 x 13 inch baking pan.

In a separate bowl, stir together the butter or coconut oil, oats, flour, brown sugar, salt, and cinnamon. Spread evenly over the berries in the baking pan.

Bake for 35–40 minutes in the baking pan until berries are bubbling vigorously. Remove from oven and let cool on wire rack in pans for at least 1 hour before serving.

Top slices of pie with a big scoop (or two) of your favorite gluten-free ice cream!

Tips for friends and family with gluten allergies

What is gluten anyway?

Gluten is a protein found in wheat, barley, and rye. It's what makes dough stretchy, helps it to rise and keep shape, and often gives foods their chewy texture.

Did you know?

Gluten is sticky. The word *gluten* comes from Latin, meaning "glue"!

Can't have gluten? Here are some helpful tips for being gluten-free:

* Focus on what your child can eat, not what he or she can't eat.

* Make it fun—let your kids be part of the menu-planning and cooking process.

* Keep your child's classroom stocked with a gluten-free snack, such as fruit gummies, for class parties when treats that contain gluten are provided. That way your child knows ahead of time that he, too, will have a yummy treat during the party.

* When dining out, call the restaurant and check the menu ahead of time. Often the restaurant will have their menu available to view online. If it does not, explain your situation to the manager when you arrive and make sure they are willing to work with you.

* Be careful of soy. When looking for food made without gluten, often products will replace gluten with soy. However, soy can often be cross-contaminated by wheat and may contain gluten. This goes for oats too. Oats are often grown in rotation with gluten crops.

* Look for a certified gluten-free seal on food products. So many products now carry these labels that it's become easier to find these foods. Gluten-free certification programs require food manufacturers to follow strict sourcing guidelines for their raw materials, which means the end products will contain less cross-contamination too.

* There are many great substitutes for regular flour including rice flour, corn flour, flaxseed flour, and more.

* Make sure your allergic child doesn't borrow a sibling's or a friend's utensils to avoid accidentally eating gluten.

* When washing dishes, use separate sponges for gluten-free and gluten dishes.

* Whether your child is gluten intolerant or not, when hosting a party for your child, avoid all treats that could be problematic and give out balloons instead!

Helpful websites and resources

celiac.com/gluten-free
A celiac disease and gluten-free forum

celiaccentral.org/kids

celiacdisease.about.com

eatingglutenfree.com

glutenfreely.com

glutenfreeville.com

glutenfreeworks.com

fda.gov
Provides information about food labeling

Sue Fliess is the author of numerous children's books. She lives in the San Francisco Bay Area with her husband, two sons, and their big yellow lab, Teddy. She loves traveling, reading, writing, and all kinds of cake—especially the birthday kind. To see all of Sue's books, please visit www.suefliess.com.

Jennifer E. Morris is an award-winning children's book illustrator. Her work has appeared in numerous children's books and publications, including *May I Please Have a Cookie?* and *Please Write Back!* both of which she wrote. Growing up in Pennsylvania, Jennifer always wanted a backyard birthday party, but since her birthday is in January, it would have been hard to find the piñata candy in the snow!

Library of Congress Cataloging-in-Publication Data

Fliess, Sue.
A gluten-free birthday for me! / Sue Fliess ; illustrated by Jennifer Morris.
pages cm
Summary: Simple, rhyming text describes a birthday celebration that starts with finding the perfect recipe for a gluten-free cake. Includes recipes, tips for people with gluten allergies, and a list of web sites for more information.
ISBN 978-0-8075-2955-3 (hardback)
[1. Stories in rhyme. 2. Gluten-free diet—Fiction. 3. Birthday cakes—Fiction. 4. Birthday parties—Fiction.]
I. Morris, Jennifer, illustrator. II. Title.
PZ8.3.F642Glu 2013
[E]—dc23
2013005443

Text copyright © 2013 Sue Fliess • Illustrations copyright © 2013 Jennifer E. Morris
Published in 2013 by Albert Whitman & Company

Printed in China.
10 9 8 7 6 5 4 3 2 1 NP 18 17 16 15 14 13

Designed by Stephanie Bart-Horvath

For more information about Albert Whitman & Company,
visit our web site at www.albertwhitman.com.